MW00935888

The Wishing Stone
#1 Dangerous Dinosaur

By: Lorana Hoopes

Illustrated by: Kendall "Mavis" Jackson

Copyright © 2017 Lorana Hoopes

Published by H&H Publishing

All rights reserved.

ISBN: 1544621175
ISBN-13: 978-1544621173

DEDICATION

This book is dedicated first and foremost to my children who are the characters and inspiration for my stories and then to all the young readers out there looking for a good story. I hope you enjoy reading this book as much I enjoyed writing it.

CONTENTS

ACKNOWLEDGMENTS

Thank you to the wonderful moms and kids who beta read this for me and let me know they enjoyed it. Thank you Kathy, Joann, Natalie, Misty, Amber, Kim, and everyone who read.

Be sure to visit https://twoheartbeats.org to get a free audio reading of this book from author Lorana Hoopes.

Follow the journey with Book 2: Dragon Dilemma and Book 3: Mesmerizing Mermaids (coming September 2017)

1 THE STRANGER

Spenser kicked a stone as he exited the school building, his shoulders low beneath the weight of the teacher's announcement. He had to read an entire book by Friday and do a book report on it. He had never read an entire book before, and he didn't want to start now. He wanted to go home and play his new computer game. It had zombies and ninjas, every boy's dream, but he knew his mother would never let him play when she found out about this homework. She would make him sit at the kitchen table and read, so she could watch him while she prepared dinner.

His mother always made him sit at the table to do homework, and he hated it. The chair wasn't comfortable, and under her watchful eye, he wasn't allowed to rush through assignments. Plus, he could usually hear the low hum of the television as his little sister, Kayleigh, and his brother, Jackson, watched Paw Patrol or Sofia the First. That only made his punishment feel worse. Sometimes he hated being the oldest.

He kicked another rock, sending it shooting down the path. It landed in front of a pair of dark brown boots. Spenser raised his head to see a man dressed in a dark brown coat and boots standing a few feet in front of him. His skin was pale, making his dark garments look even more like night. On his head perched a brown cowboy hat. It hung low over his eyes, so Spenser couldn't make out much of his face.

Spenser looked to the left and right, clutching the straps of his backpack tighter. He had read about cowboys but never seen one in real life. There weren't many in western Washington. His mother, who was from Texas, spoke of them occasionally, but even she said there weren't as many as there used to be.

"Why you looking so glum little pardner?" the man drawled. His accent was heavy, and his words were slow.

Spenser wasn't supposed to talk to strangers, but his curiosity got the best of him. "I have to read a book and do a report on it by Friday, and I don't like reading."

"Well, that is a mighty big problem," the man agreed, tipping his hat. "Maybe you just ain't found the right book yet."

"What do you mean?" Spenser asked, narrowing his eyes at the man.

"Books can be full of amazing stories. Once you find one you like, I'll bet you'll be hooked for life pardner. Here, I got something that might help." He reached into the pocket of his brown duster and pulled something out. It was small enough to fit in his hand.

Unable to help himself, Spenser took another step closer. His blue eyes widened as he waited for the man to open his hand.

The man's fingers uncurled one at a time to showcase . .

"A rock?" Spenser's nose wrinkled in disgust. He had

been hoping for something cooler than a rock.

"Not just any rock, son. This is a wishing stone. You jest

hold it while you read and see what happens, but I must warn

4

you to be careful of your thoughts. For sometimes, when you hold this stone, magical things happen."

Spenser looked again at the stone. Though nearly completely white, it still looked just like an ordinary rock to him. He took the rock, expecting nothing, but a cool sensation tickled up his arms. He glanced up quickly at the man, who merely smiled and nodded, as if they now shared a secret.

"Jest remember to hold that while you read," the man said. He tipped his hat one more time and then walked away.

Spenser was left holding the rock and wondering about the man. He didn't believe that anything special would happen when he held the rock, but the tingle that had gone up his arms was strange. It was fading now, but he could still feel a small remnant of the chill. He supposed it couldn't hurt to try. After tucking the rock in his front pocket, Spenser continued to his house.

2 THE BOOK

"**B**rudder," Kayleigh said, running up to Spenser as he walked in the door. Kayleigh was not quite two, so her words were still not always clear, but her pixie blond hair and blue eyes made her irresistible all the same.

"Hi, Kayleigh." Spenser patted her head, which was his normal greeting and continued into the kitchen.

Jackson, his four-year-old little brother, sat at the kid's table eating a snack of goldfish.

"Hey, honey, how was your day?" his mother asked as she looked up from the sink where she was washing dishes.

"It was okay," Spenser said, dropping his backpack on the table. "I have to read a book and do a report."

"Well, it will be good for you," his mother said. "I used to love to read. Hopefully, you will find a book you enjoy too."

"Can you take me to the library?" he asked as the idea popped into his head. If he was going to have to read, he wanted something different than the baby books in the house.

She looked at her watch. "Sure, we can do that." His mother picked up Kayleigh, grabbed her keys, and motioned for Jackson to join them.

After making sure everyone was buckled in, his mother started the car and a few minutes later, they were all tumbling out again into the parking lot of the local library.

The library was a small brick building overlooking a duck pond. It didn't seem large from the outside, but the inside appeared huge to Spenser. Rows and rows of shelves filled the room and each shelf held books from one end to the other.

His mother led them to the kids' book section, but Spenser wanted to try something else. He wanted to see if he could find a book about dinosaurs. At least those interested him.

After explaining to his mom what he wanted, she stated they could probably find a dinosaur story in the kid section and she helped him look. A small chapter book with a caveman and a large green dinosaur caught his attention. Arco and the Dangerous Dinosaur read the cover.

"This one, Mom, please?" he asked, holding it out

to her.

"That's fine, son."

They spent a few more minutes looking for a book about trains for Jackson and one about princesses for Kayleigh. Then they joined the line at the front desk.

Spenser got a new library card and checked out his first book on his own card, while his mother checked out the other two books on her card. Though he liked dinosaurs, he was more interested in seeing what the stone might do as he read.

As they walked back to the car, Spenser could barely contain his excitement. He wanted to open the book and grab the stone to see what would happen, but he made himself keep the book closed the entire ride home.

His mother parked the car and began unbuckling his brother and sister from their car seats. "Spenser, go sit at the table as you read, so I can cook dinner," his mother said as they entered the house.

"But mom," he whined.

"No buts young man."

Sighing, Spenser sat at the table and opened his book. The book was about a boy named Arco who was being asked to defend his village from a terrible dinosaur. While the story seemed interesting, Spenser couldn't focus because his finger itched to touch the stone.

"If I promise to read, can I please read in my room?" Spenser asked.

His mother opened her mouth as if to say no, but as Kayleigh was at her feet crying to be picked up and Jackson was running back and forth wanting to show off toys, she changed her mind and said yes.

Delighted, Spenser closed the book and ran up the carpeted stairs. Once in his room, he climbed atop his bed and opened the book again. This time as he read, he fingered the smooth white stone. "I wish I could meet

Arco," he said softly, and the room around him began to change.

3 THE ADVENTURE

When the room finally stopped shaking, Spenser found himself outside a small mud hut. Several other mud huts created a large circle. People scurried back and forth wearing some sort of animal skins and furs. A large campfire was lit in the middle of the circle. Children sat in front of it warming themselves, and a few adults held sticks into the fire that contained some sort of meat on the end.

"Whoa," Spenser whispered softly. "This looks just like the picture of Arco's village." He pocketed the stone he still held in his hand and stepped forward from the

shadows. A small boy saw him. His eyes grew wide and he

pointed at Spenser.

"Intruder," he yelled.

Immediately, Spenser was surrounded by grown men

and women pointing spears in his direction.

"Wait," he yelled, holding his hands up. "I'm just

looking for Arco. I'm here to help, I think."

Though the people looked at him warily, they did not

move any farther with their spears. Suddenly, a boy who

looked just a few years older than Spenser appeared in the

crowd. He had long brown hair and his skin was darker

than Spenser's. An animal skin tunic hung from his

shoulders to just above his knees.

"I am Arco. Who are you? Where did you come

from?"

"I am Spenser. I come from the future. At least I think it's the future. I was reading of your problem, and I think I was sent here to help."

The boy's eyebrows knitted together. "You? How can you help?"

"I don't know," Spenser replied, "but I'm willing to try and find out."

Arco stared at him a moment longer. His mouth opened, but before he could speak the ground began to shake and a terrible roar filled the air.

"Quick, to the huts," Arco yelled. He grabbed

Spenser's arm and pulled him into the nearest hut.

Spenser held his hands over his ears, trying to stop the

noise that was causing his teeth to chatter against his will.

He could feel the roar in his head. "What is that?" he

yelled to Arco.

"*That* is our problem," the boy yelled back.

Suddenly a large leg covered in green filled the view of the small window. Spenser heard himself scream, but because the roaring was so loud, he doubted anyone else did. The people, Spenser included, bounced like rubber balls against the earthen floor with each step the creature took.

After another few howls and a close call from the giant tail sweeping near the hut they stood in, the creature began to move away from the village. The hearing in Spenser's ears slowly came back. He rubbed his backside which ached from the pounding it had taken falling on the ground so many times.

"That was the dinosaur," Arco continued as he surveyed the damage of the camp. "He comes every few days. Sometimes he just steps on our fire like now, but he has knocked over a few of our huts and people have been injured. We must find a way to stop him. Do you have any ideas?"

Spenser racked his brain, but he was only a boy. He wished he had read more of the book before touching the stone so maybe he would have an idea of how to help. "Is there a way we can watch him the next time he comes?" Spenser asked.

"Watch him? Why would we want to do that?" Arco asked.

"Well creatures can't talk with words, but sometimes they show us what they need by their actions," Spenser said, remembering his cat at home who always pawed at his leg when she wanted his attention.

Arco nodded in understanding. "You are saying that maybe he doesn't come to destroy our village, but he comes seeking some help with something?"

"I don't know for sure," Spenser replied, "but it's worth a shot."

"What does worth a shot mean?" Arco asked, his forehead wrinkling in confusion.

"A try," Spenser explained, wondering how the people could speak as well as he did but not know some of his words.

Arco nodded, and he and Spenser began to help pick up the destruction left behind by the dinosaur. A few people helped relight the campfire and Spenser joined Arco around the fire.

Arco offered a piece of meat to Spenser, but though his stomach rumbled, he did not take it as he wasn't sure what the food was and his adventurous spirit ended at trying new foods. He did, however, take some bread, which while heavier than his normal wheat bread at home, was very good.

"This isn't how I thought cave people lived at all," Spenser said to Arco.

"We no longer live in caves," Arco said between bites. "It got too dark, and we enjoyed the light outside. So, we created these huts."

"How do you stay safe from dinosaurs? Don't they attack often?" Spenser thought back to an old TV show he used to watch where a family lived in a cave to avoid dinosaur attacks.

"There are only a few who come after us. Most around here are peaceful vegetable eaters. They are our friends. When the meat eaters come, we can usually hide in the huts, which mask our scent, but there are a few caves in the hillside we can return to if we must."

"How do you know so many words?" Spenser asked. "All the shows I watched of cavemen show them only knowing one or two words like 'fire good.'"

"I do not know how to answer your question," Arco said. "We speak as we have always spoken."

Spenser nodded as he ate another bite of bread. He wondered what his family was doing right now? Had they even noticed he was gone or did time stand still while he was here?

"Come, let us rest," Arco said as he finished his meat. "Tomorrow we can go look for the dinosaur."

Spenser followed Arco back into the mud hut they had hidden in. Arco handed him two furs, one to lay on the floor and the other to cover up with. Spenser curled up with his furs, but sleep eluded him. What if they couldn't stop the dinosaur? Would he ever make it back home?

4 THE HUNT

The next morning Spenser woke to Arco nudging him. "Come on, the dinosaur is close. Let us go see if we can find out more information."

Spenser threw back the fur that was covering him and stood. His body was stiff from sleeping on the ground, and he had to stretch a few times before he could stand completely straight. Once his body would follow his commands, he trailed Arco out of the hut.

Arco put a few pieces of dried meat, which looked a lot like beef jerky, in a sort of leather pouch, along with some bread and some round objects that resembled fruit, though not like any Spenser had seen before. A few other young men carrying spears joined them and they set out from the village.

They entered a forest that looked a lot like the forests back home except that it seemed much greener and animals he had only seen in books hurried back and forth. A loud flapping noise pulled his attention upward and Spenser saw a large grey pterodactyl fly above their heads.

The forest opened into a clearing and Spenser gasped. Huge four-legged dinosaurs grazed on trees, their long necks gracefully reaching to the top. Suddenly the ground began shaking again, followed by the same loud wail from the previous night. The grazing dinosaurs stopped munching and began moving away.

"Take cover," Arco yelled, and dragged Spenser

behind a large tree. The other few boys hid among the

larger rocks. A minute later, the large green dinosaur

stomped into view. Spenser was surprised to see feathers

on the dinosaur. It didn't look like any dinosaur he had

ever seen. It looked like a cross between a bird and a

dinosaur. He'd have to remember to ask Arco about it

later.

Spenser again covered his ears, though it didn't lessen

the sound much. The dinosaur shook his head back and

forth. His tiny front hands fluttered as if trying to reach his

head, but they were much too short. The dinosaur scraped

his head against a tree before letting out another large

wail. He turned his head to the left and right, then

stomped out of the clearing

"It looks like he's in pain," Spenser said when the noise was far enough away that he could remove his hands from his ears.

"What?" Arco asked.

"He looked like he was trying to reach his head, but his hands were too small. And the way he scraped his head against the trees makes me think he is in pain and is trying to find a way to relieve it."

"How do we get close enough to find out the issue though?" Arco asked.

Spenser looked around. There was no mountain here, but in the distance, he could see one rising. "How far is that mountain?" he asked pointing.

"A good day's walk," Arco said. "What are you thinking?"

"If we can get high enough, maybe we can see what is bothering the dinosaur's head," Spenser said.

Arco's mouth pursed as he thought. Then his dark eyes lit up. "About an hour from here is a lookout. It might be tall enough."

"Let's go then," Spenser said and he followed Arco and the other boys out of the clearing. "That dinosaur didn't look like the ones in my book. Do all dinosaurs have feathers?"

"Most do, or some fuzz covering them. It helps them stay warm. They do not show feathers in your books?"

"No, but I'll have to do more research when I get home," Spenser said. *(research in reference section)

When they arrived at the lookout an hour later, Spenser's feet were sore. He wondered how Arco and the boys walked so far with such thin soles on their feet.

"There it is," Arco said.

Spenser looked up. A tall tree had knots growing out of its trunk that looked like perfect handholds, and the branches were missing enough leaves that they would make good seats. He wasn't sure it was tall enough, but it was higher than they had been before.

Arco climbed the tree quickly and motioned for the others to follow. Spenser wasn't sure he could climb as fast as the other boys, but he was not afraid of heights, so he knew he could make it to the top.

He was careful to make sure his hands had a good grip before he moved his feet. Then he made sure his feet were steady before he moved his hands. He wasn't sure what would happen to him if he got injured in this world, but he didn't want to find out.

Finally, he reached the top and inched out on the branch to sit next to Arco. From up here, he could see the village in the distance and many more dinosaurs. He scanned for the green dinosaur, finally spotting it to the left.

"How do we get it to come here?" Spenser asked

Arco.

Arco smiled and pulled a hollowed-out horn from his

pouch. "We call him," Arco said, putting the horn to his

lips and blowing. A low sound came out of the horn, but

the green dinosaur didn't move any closer. Arco blew the

horn again, louder this time, and Spenser saw the

dinosaur's head lift and turn their direction. The ground

began to shake as the dinosaur grew closer. Spenser

clutched the branch tighter to keep from falling off.

The dinosaur broke into the area where the lookout

was. From this height, Spenser could see his huge teeth.

"Maybe this was a bad idea," he muttered.

"No, look," Arco pointed.

Above the dinosaur's eye was a large branch. It

appeared lodged in his skin.

"I bet he's trying to get that out," Arco said.

"But how do we help him?" Spenser asked. The boys

all shook their heads. None of them knew.

When the dinosaur finally left the area, the boys

climbed down and returned to the village. They were silent

on the return trip, trying to think of a way to help the

dinosaur.

5 THE PLAN

Spenser joined Arco and the others around the fire. This time Spenser did try the meat, which tasted a lot like chicken. As they ate, they shared with the others what they had learned.

"Could we build a contraption?" Spenser asked. "Something to remove the twig?"

Arco shook his head. "We have very limited tools."

"I don't suppose anyone would be strong enough to pull it out," Spenser suggested.

"Even if they were, how would they get high enough to reach it?" Arco asked.

A silence fell.

"Do we have any way to put the dinosaur to sleep?" Spenser asked. "If so, we could all pull the branch out while he's sleeping."

"Hmm," Arco said. "Perhaps the old woman can mix something together."

"The old woman?" Spenser asked.

"She's the village healer. She mixes herbs to make potions and poultices. Perhaps she can mix something together to make a sleeping potion. But she is a little crazy."

"Is she here in town?" Spenser asked.

"No, just outside of town."

"Let's go then," Spenser said, standing.

"No, not in the dark. We'll go first thing in the morning."

Spenser sighed. As much fun as he was having, he had to wonder if his family was looking for him. Had they called the police? Was Kayleigh walking around the house hollering "brudder" as she looked for him? Was Jackson scouring the room for a playmate? Was anyone crying for him to come home? The thoughts kept him up for several hours that night.

When the sun rose the next morning, Arco again packed some food. He and Spenser set out to go visit the old woman.

"Be sure to let me do the talking," Arco said.

"Of course," Spenser agreed. "What should I be expecting?"

"Don't stare at her face," Arco began. "It is hideous, but she doesn't like it when you stare. Also, the last time I saw her, she was very filthy. Are you afraid of rats?"

"Uh, I'm not sure. I've never seen one in real life," Spenser said.

"Well, you may today," Arco said. "Try not to scream."

Spenser nodded, wondering if he would be able to stay calm when he saw the old woman.

A dark mud hut appeared in the forest. It was surrounded by lush greenery, but that didn't make it look any brighter.

Spenser followed Arco into the hut. His heart was pounding in his chest.

"Old woman?" Arco called.

Was that her only name? Spenser wondered.

"Who's there?" The voice that came back was deep and throaty, like a frog.

"It's Arco and my friend Spenser from another time."

A short woman with long white hair came around the corner. She had a large nose with a wart on the end. One long silver hair grew out of the wart and three more sprouted from her chin. Both eyes were filmy and watery. She was indeed a very unattractive woman.

"What can I do for you?" she asked. When she opened her mouth, Spenser could see that she only had about four teeth left and each pointed in a different direction.

"We need a sleeping potion. Can you make such a thing?" Arco asked.

"Depends on who you are trying to put to sleep," the woman cackled.

Spenser tore his gaze away, trying not to stare at her. A large furry rat ran across the woman's feet and Spenser jumped back. The woman appeared not to notice.

"We need to put a dinosaur to sleep," Arco said. Spenser wondered how he could remain so calm.

"That would be a lot of potion," the woman said.

"I brought you enough food for a week as payment," Arco said, holding out the bag.

The woman swiped the bag and pawed through it. Grunting in agreement, she tossed the bag onto a small brown table littered with bowls and old bits of food. More rats ran across the table as their hiding spaces were revealed.

The old woman waddled over to a hole in the wall where a large black pot hung from a pole. A fire burned beneath the pot. "Let's see," she said, reaching for small vials atop a shelf near the pot. "We'll need some Lavender and some Bane's breath." She poured a little of each into the large pot. "And of course, some toxic mushrooms to keep him still while he sleeps. Not too much though, we don't want to kill him, right?" She cackled again and the hair on the back of Spenser's neck rose on end. "And the final ingredient, that one is a secret of course."

As she put the last ingredient in, a puff of purple smoke rose in the air.

"It just needs a few minutes to cook," the woman said. "Go get me an empty vial from over there." She pointed to the other side of the room where another shelf hung on the wall. Bottles of all shapes and sizes sat on the shelf, but the pathway to it was filled with more clutter. Arco gracefully stepped around the clutter and plucked a vial from the shelf. It was perhaps six inches high and fat at the bottom though it narrowed at the top. He stepped

lightly back through the minefield that was her floor and

handed the vial to her.

She took a sniff of the potion and then picked up a

ladle and poured some into the vial. She continued

pouring until the vial was full. Then she pulled a brown

cork from a pocket in her dress and capped the bottle.

"You boy," she said to Spenser, "Come here."

Spenser looked at Arco, who nodded his head to show it was okay. Then he stepped closer to the old woman, who handed the bottle to him.

"Be sure to use all of it or else he may not stay asleep as long as you need him to," the woman said. "Best of luck to you."

"Thank you," Spenser said and Arco echoed and performed a little bow before exiting the hut. Spenser quickly followed, still clutching the bottle for fear of breaking it.

Once outside, he handed the bottle to Arco, who tucked it in a small leather bag he had slung over one shoulder.

"Do you think it will work?" Spenser asked.

"We can only hope," Arco replied. "But we have nothing to lose."

They continued the short trek back to the village and then gathered a group together to discuss how best to put the potion on the dinosaur.

"There is the tall tree," Arco pointed out. "Someone could stand at the top and pour the potion on the dinosaur when he comes by."

"That sounds very dangerous," an older man said.

"I can do it," Spenser said.

"No, I can do it," Arco said. "I appreciate your help, but you are not from here. It should be one of us who does it."

"Let's do it together," Spenser said and Arco agreed.

6 THE DINOSAUR SLEEPS

Later that afternoon, Arco and Spenser climbed the tall tree. Arco had his horn in the small pouch along with the vial. When they reached the top, they picked a strong branch to climb out on.

"Be sure to watch which way the dinosaur leans once he is asleep," Arco hollered down to the people below. "He might hit some of the huts depending on how he falls, so be ready to get the people out."

The men and women below nodded.

"Thank you for this friend," Arco said holding out a hand to Spenser. "You barely know us and you are willing to risk your life to help us."

"I think you would do the same for me if the tables were turned," Spenser said and shook Arco's hand.

Arco nodded, a smile stretching across his face. "It would be my honor to. Are you ready?"

Spenser nodded and Arco lifted the horn to his lips. The deep sound bellowed out and Spenser waited. Only the sound of the leaves rustling in the wind met Spenser's ears. Arco blew the horn again. Suddenly the tree began to shake. The ferocious howl met their ears and Spenser clutched the branch tighter. The people below began to take cover behind large rocks and smaller trees.

The green dinosaur broke into the village. His tiny hands clawed back and forth and his head shook left and right. His tail sent swirls of dust up into the air.

Beside him, Arco dropped the horn into the bag and removed the vial. He uncapped it. Spenser could see the bottle shaking just slightly in Arco's hand. For all his bravery, he must be a little nervous, Spenser thought.

The dinosaur lumbered their direction and Spenser grabbed ahold of Arco's tunic. It had been decided that Arco would lean out and drop the potion on the dinosaur while Spenser held onto him and the tree. His life was in Spenser's hands.

"Just a little closer," Arco said as the dinosaur stepped toward them again. Spenser could now see the reptilian eye looking back and forth and the branch still lodged above the eye. As he took one more step and ended up next to the tree, Arco leaned forward and flung the potion at the dinosaur.

It hit him directly in the nose and the dinosaur reared its head, letting out another loud roar. His hands clawed again and his eyes looked around, landing on Spenser and Arco in the tree. He took a step toward them and Spenser squeezed his eyes shut, expecting to be knocked from the tree and tumble to his death.

Instead he heard Arco yell, "Clear the right side."

Spenser opened his eyes to see people below running out of the mud huts on the right side of the circle. The dinosaur's eyes were starting to close and he was leaning to the right. He stumbled out of the village, narrowly missing a house, and into the tall grassy area that lay just beyond the village huts. With a giant thud, he collapsed. His head had landed on a boulder, and it now looked almost like a pillow under his large head. The tall grass was almost like a blanket covering part of his massive body.

"We did it," Spenser said, his voice full of awe.

"Yes, we did," Argo agreed. "But now we must see if we can get the branch out before the dinosaur awakes."

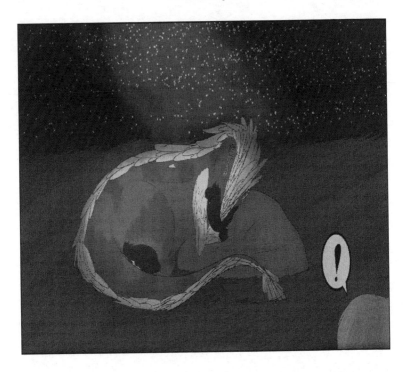

Spenser and Arco made their way back down the tree

and joined the crowd that had gathered around the

dinosaur. The branch was large and sticking out of the eye

closest to the ground.

"Get some rope," Arco yelled to the crowd. A few

scattered off to find a long piece of rope. When they

returned, Arco climbed up on a nearby rock and tied the

rope around the branch. He made sure to secure it behind

a small piece that jutted out and would hold the rope in place.

"Grab ahold of the rope and let's pull," Arco said as he climbed down from the rock. He flung the rope out to the crowd, and men and women stepped forward to grab a portion. Spenser wrapped his hands around a bit of rope near Arco. The rope was slick, and he couldn't get the best hold, but he held on as tight as he could. On Arco's count, they began to pull.

At first, Spenser felt nothing, but little by little, he felt the branch shift. A few more tugs and the branch came free, sending people sprawling across the ground as they lost their footing. Those still holding on carried the branch away from the crowd and laid it down gently.

"Did it work?" one woman asked.

"We will have to wait and see if that was the problem," Arco said. "Be sure to keep an eye on the dinosaur. We may need to run quickly if that was not the issue."

The crowd murmured in agreement, and Spenser and Arco sat down together on a nearby boulder to wait.

"Why do they listen to you?" Spenser asked. "You seem young like me."

"I am twelve years old," Arco said. "My father was the chief of this village, but was killed on a hunt."

"I'm sorry," Spenser said. He couldn't imagine how he would feel if he didn't have his dad.

"I had to take over in his place," Arco continued. "They listen to me because I am now the chief."

"Isn't that a lot of work for someone so young?" Spenser asked.

Arco nodded. "It is, but we do not always get to choose our path. Sometimes fate chooses it for us."

Spenser thought about that. Had fate sent him the mysterious stranger? Was he on a path other than the one he would have chosen? His family flashed into his mind and he found he missed them. He hoped the stone would take him back when the quest was complete because he had no other way of getting home. He should have asked the stranger more questions. He shouldn't have tried the stone without knowing he had a way to get home.

7 A NEW FRIEND

It was hours later when the dinosaur finally began to move. Spenser and Arco were eating a dinner of meat and bread again when the cry sounded.

"It's waking up," a man yelled.

All around them, the men, women, and children got to their feet. Mothers grabbed their children and held them tight about the shoulders, ready to bolt if the dinosaur appeared to still be determined to destroy their village. Men held spears at the ready in a loose circle around the dinosaur in case defense was needed. Spenser and Arco stepped through the circle and close to the beast lying on

the ground. The tall grass came up to Spenser's waist.

The dinosaur's skin was leathery looking like the

elephants Spenser had seen at the zoo last year, only it

was a dark green. His large belly, slightly lighter in color,

rose and fell as he breathed. All along his back were rows

of bright red feathers. Spenser wanted to touch the

dinosaur, to see what he felt like, but he was afraid the beast might bite him.

As the dinosaur struggled to stand, Arco and Spenser stopped and watched. Though they wanted to help, they didn't really have a way to, and they were afraid to get too close.

When the dinosaur finally got to its feet, it shook its head left and right. It tilted its head up and down. The tiny hands pawed the air, but their movement was different this time. There was less anger behind the movement. The dinosaur looked down at the crowd around it. Spenser was pretty sure dinosaurs couldn't smile, but that's what his mouth looked like.

The dinosaur leaned its head down into the crowd and waited. Arco took a step toward the creature and then another. He held out his hand and the dinosaur sniffed at it. Spenser waited for the massive jaws to open, but the mouth stayed close. Instead, the dinosaur leaned his head toward Arco, like a dog wanting to be petted. Arco touched a hand on the dinosaur and smiled. Unable to contain his curiosity any longer, Spenser took the few steps needed to put him next to Arco and he too reached out a hand. The dinosaur's skin was cool like a snake, but not scaly.

"I think we have done it," Arco whispered to Spenser and Spenser nodded, still amazed that he was touching a dinosaur.

One by one the people lowered their spears and came forward. Soon everyone in the village was touching the dinosaur. The creature stayed still and let the people come. When everyone had had their turn, the dinosaur finally stood again. It let out a roar, but one that didn't sound angry this time. Then it lumbered away into the forest.

"Thank you, my friend," Arco said, turning to Spenser. "You have helped save our village."

"You're welcome," Spenser returned. Then his face fell.

"What is wrong?" Arco asked.

"As fun as this has been," Spenser said, "I miss my family, and I want to go home."

"How did you get here?" Arco asked. "Perhaps you can return the same way."

"I wished to meet you as I held this stone." Spenser pulled the stone out of his front pocket and held it up.

"Then perhaps you can wish to return home and it will take you," Arco said.

Spenser nodded, though he was a little afraid to try. What if the rock didn't work? What if it only worked with books? Could he write a book about home to return that way? Taking a deep breath, he squeezed the rock tightly in his right hand and closed his eyes. I wish to go home, he thought to himself.

The tingling shot up his arm and Spenser's eyes snapped open. The world of Arco's village was fading away. Arco raised a hand in a wave and then he was gone and Spenser was back in his bedroom, the book open in front of him.

"Whoa," he said. "I wonder how long I've been gone."

Slamming the book shut, he jammed the rock back in his pocket and looked up at his wall. He had a poster of a T-Rex hanging in front of him, but suddenly it didn't look right.

Spenser grabbed a red pen and colored a row of feathers on the dinosaur's head and back.

When he finished, he leaned back, smiling at his handiwork. Then, he opened his door to find his family. No one was in the hallway, but he could hear the television downstairs.

As he bounded into the kitchen, the smell of spaghetti met his nose.

"Oh good, it's dinnertime," his mother said.

"How long have I been gone?" Spenser asked.

"Gone?" His mother asked. "You mean reading? About an hour, I guess." She scooped out a spoonful of noodles coated in red sauce and plopped it onto a plate, holding it out to him. "Go sit at the table for dinner."

Spenser took the plate, his mind focused on what his mother had said. Only an hour? It had been days in Arco's world. Smiling, he sat down at the table.

"What are you smiling about?" Jackson asked.

"I'll tell you later," Spenser said. "It's a secret."

Thankfully Jackson didn't keep asking as Spenser's mom, dad, and Kayleigh joined them at the table.

"Did you finish your book?" his mother asked.

"Yes, it was great," Spenser said. "We'll definitely have to get some more."

His mother's eyes sparkled as she smiled. "I knew it would take just finding the right book," she said.

Or the right stone, Spenser thought. He reached down and touched the rock in his pocket, smiling to himself. He couldn't wait to go on his next adventure.

The End!

A Look At The Wishing Stone

#2: Dragon Dilemma

1 THE TROUBLE WITH SIBLINGS

Spenser stared at the clock on the wall, willing it to be 3:15. He couldn't wait to go home and try out his wishing stone again. He had only gotten to use it once since receiving it, and he was aching to try it again.

A week ago, Spenser had come across a mysterious stranger on his way home from school. The man, after hearing that Spenser didn't like to read, had offered him a white stone. The man had said that magical things would happen when Spenser held the stone while reading.

Spenser hadn't believed the mysterious stranger at first, but then Spenser had held the stone and wished to meet Arco, the character in the book he had been reading, and had been transported back to dinosaur time, where he got to see a T-rex up close. That had been amazing.

Since then, he had been begging his mother to take him back to the library to get another book. Finally, yesterday, she had agreed, and at home on his bed right now was <u>Merlin and the Dragon</u>. Spenser loved magic and dragons, so he was excited not only to read this book but to visit Merlin himself.

The bell finally rang and Spenser bounded out of his seat. He slung his backpack over his shoulders and headed for the door.

"Hey, you want to ride bikes?" his friend Zane asked.

Spenser was torn. He did want to ride bikes and he had just gotten a new bike for Christmas, but he really wanted to try the stone again. It was in his pocket right now, and his fingers itched to touch it.

"I can't tonight, but do you want to ride tomorrow?"

Zane's face grew sad for a moment before lighting up at the prospect of a meeting tomorrow. "Sure, that will be fun."

Spenser waved goodbye and started towards home. He didn't live very far, so he walked to and from school. The path went through a little park and kept him away from the streets. Every day, he kept his eyes peeled for the mysterious stranger. He hadn't seen him again, but he hoped to. For one, he wanted to thank the man for the magical rock, but he also wanted to see if the man had any other magical items.

There was no luck today, either. He did not spot the man on his walk home.

Spenser opened the green front door of his house and called out to his mother. "Mom, I'm home."

"In the kitchen, honey," came her reply.

He tossed his backpack by the door and headed that way, but before he had even rounded the corner, Kayleigh appeared, hugging his legs.

"Brudder," she said, smiling up at him.

"Hi, Kayleigh. Did you have a fun day today?"

"Yesh," she said, her little blond head nodding up and down.

When she finally released his leg, he continued into the kitchen. His mother sat at the table with Jackson, showing him how to write the letter D.

"Spenser, look," Jackson said, holding up his picture. "D is for dragon." Jackson was just as fascinated by dragons as Spenser was.

"It's nice," Spenser said. His hand patted his pocket. How much longer would he have to stay down here before he could sneak up to his room?

"Do you have homework, Spenser?" his mother asked.

This was his chance. "Just some reading, mom. Can I go upstairs to read?"

"Sure," his mother agreed. "I'll call you when it's time for dinner."

Barely able to contain his excitement, Spenser turned around and bounded up the stairs.

He threw open his door. The book called to him from his bed, and in his haste, he forgot to shut the door behind him. Climbing up on the bed, he sat cross legged, his back to the door, and opened the book.

He didn't see Jackson and Kayleigh sneak into the room behind him.

Be sure to get the rest of Book 2 to continue the journey. https://www.amazon.com/Wishing-Stone-Dragon-Dilemma/dp/1974398951/ref=tmm_pap_swatch_0?_encoding=UTF8&qid=&sr=

References and Dinosaur Facts:

New research is showing that dinosaurs might be more bird like thank we think.
http://news.nationalgeographic.com/2017/02/anchiornis-bird-like-dinosaur-feathers-lasers-soft-tissue-science/

Did T. Rex Have Feathers?
A feathered T. rex? Probably so--at least when the animals were young. Paleontologists think feathers may have first evolved to keep dinosaurs warm. But while a young T. rex probably had a thin coat of downy feathers, an adult T. rex would not have needed feathers to stay warm. Large warm-blooded animals--like T. rex or modern elephants--generate a great deal of body heat so they usually don't need hair or feathers to keep warm. This is probably why elephants, which are mammals, don't have much hair.
http://www.amnh.org/exhibitions/dinosaurs-ancient-fossils-new-discoveries/liaoning-diorama/a-feathered-tyrant/

ABOUT THE AUTHOR

Lorana Hoopes is an inspirational author who lives in the Pacific Northwest with her husband and three children. She has written three adult inspirational fiction books under The Heartbeats series: The Power of Prayer, Where It All Began, and When Hearts Collide. She is currently finishing the fourth book in the series, A Father's Love. http://bit.ly/Heartbeatcollection

Lorana decided to start a children's series after reading The Magic Tree House books with her son. While she loved that he was reading, as an English teacher, the simple sentences bothered her, so she decided to try something just a step up and The Wishing Stone series was born. Dangerous Dinosaur is the first book in the series, but be sure to stay tuned for The Dragon Dilemma out now and Mesmerizing Mermaids coming September 2017!

49349373R00047

Made in the USA
Middletown, DE
18 October 2017